D1126192   ⌐2

NORTHWEST ANIMAL
BaBies

Photographs by Art Wolfe
Written by Andrea Helman

SASQUATCH BOOKS
SEATTLE

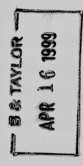

Bison Calf

Humpless, hornless, and cinnamon-colored,
a bison calf weighs over 65 pounds at birth and receives a welcoming
lick from mom. Mother cows take turns watching all the herd's calves.
If they sense danger, they stampede to safety.

Raccoon Kits

Curious raccoon kits peek out of their safe den.
See their five fingers? Raccoons use their paws and sharp claws just like
hands to feel underwater for crawdads and to scamper up tall trees.

Harbor Seal Pup

How do a harbor seal pup and its mother say hello? With their whiskers! Sometimes a pup will wait alone on the beach while mom goes into the water to catch fish. When she returns, they touch their whiskers in happy greeting.

Trumpeter Swan Cygnet

Tap! Tap! This cygnet used its eggtooth—a hard, pointed knob on its bill—to break out of its egg. It will start swimming in only two days, but a full year will pass before the cygnet turns into a beautiful white swan.

Porcupine Kit

Newborn porcupines are as soft and cuddly as other furry babies, but not for long. Their quills harden quickly after birth, making the kit prickly from its eyebrows to the tip of its tail.

Gray Wolf Pups

Gray wolf pups
live in friendly groups
called packs. While playing,
they learn to use their
powerful jaws and pointed
teeth for grabbing and holding
prey. Wolves walk in single
file through the deep
Montana snow, taking turns
breaking the trail.

Dall Sheep Lamb

Can you guess how old the mother ewe is?
Just count the rings on her horns. Dall sheep live in the rugged mountains
of Alaska and northwestern Canada. Ewes have one lamb a year,
which can walk just a few hours after birth.

Opossum Kits

At birth, opossums are no bigger than a honeybee!
They snuggle into mom's warm pouch to nurse and grow,
just like baby kangaroos. When they're big enough, they ride
on mom's back, clinging to her with their claws.

Golden Eagle Eaglet

This downy eaglet will grow up to be a large, dark-brown bird of prey with a wingspan of seven feet. Sometimes called the "mountain eagle," golden eagles nest in tall trees or on high cliffs in remote areas.

Coho Salmon Fry

Shimmering, slippery coho, also called silver salmon,
are born in freshwater streams, then migrate out to the ocean.
In open water, salmon fry look like shadows,
making it hard for predators to see them.

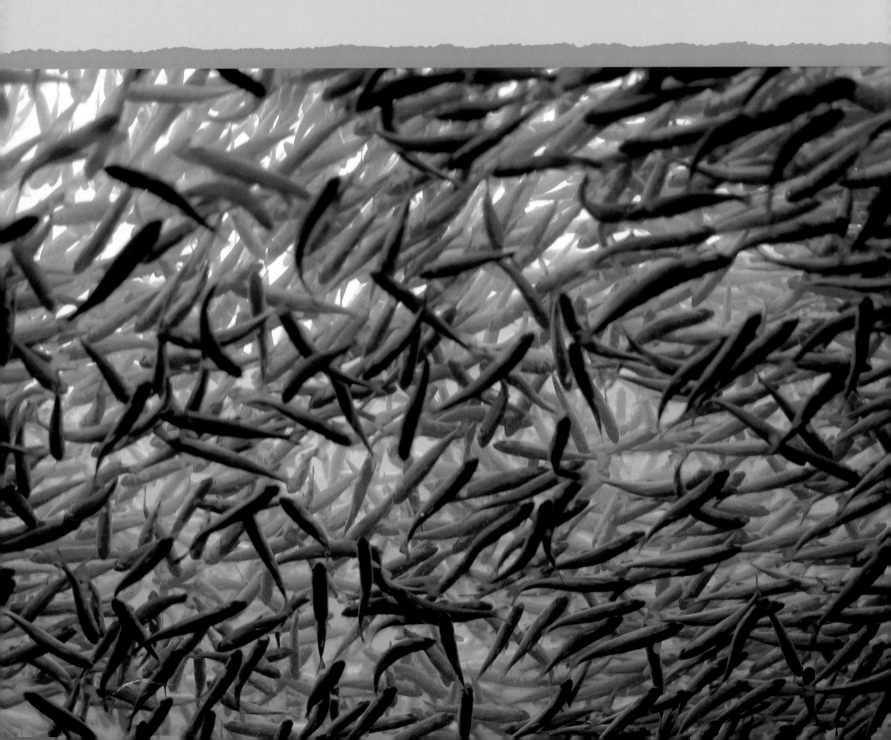

Grizzly Bear Cubs

Grizzly cubs love to climb trees, play and swim in the water,
and eat fattening salmon. They have excellent memories and never
forget where to find a berry field that mom has shown them.
If danger threatens, mom sends them up a tree until it is safe.

Mountain Goat Kid

Within a week of being born, a mountain goat kid can easily follow its mother nanny, jumping from craggy rocks to cliff ledges. Can you see the nanny's beard? It is part of a thick throat mane that helps keep her warm.

Polar Bear Cubs

Creamy white polar bears are hard to see or hear in their frozen homeland. Their paws are covered with fur for warmth, traction, and "soundproofing"—so seals under the ice can't hear them. Cubs slide down icy slopes into frigid waters, splashing and dog-paddling with their huge paws.

White-tailed Deer Fawn

A white-tailed fawn bleats like a lamb when it wants its mother, who answers in a high-pitched call that humans cannot hear. Fawns are born well-camouflaged and with almost no scent, making it difficult for predators to find them.

River Otter Pup

Mom and dad like to join their pups when they play, sledding down muddy banks and along the ice of frozen rivers. By closing its ears and nostrils, a river otter can stay under water for almost four minutes.

Bobcat Kitten

See the white spots on the back of mother's ears? Her kitten watches for these spots if it falls behind during evening hunting lessons. In only nine months, the kitten will be as big as mom.

Northwest Crow Fledglings

These crow fledglings may live up to ten years,
much longer than many birds. Curious and intelligent, crows are
excellent problem solvers. Some have learned to fly high into the
sky with a mussel, and then drop it on the rocks to break it open.

Orca Calf

An orca calf weighs 400 pounds at birth,
but is still much smaller than the adults in its family.
The baby swims just behind its mother in her "slipstream," which pulls it
along when the pod is traveling through Pacific Northwest waters.

Burrowing Owl Owlets

Not all owls are night owls, and these sleepy owlets are glad to soak up the morning sun. Yawn! Burrowing owls live in underground nests in eastern Washington. When they feel threatened, they don't hoot like other owls, but squeak and squawk.

Blue-winged Teal Ducklings

Blue-winged teal ducklings are born into big families.
Can you imagine having as many as 15 brothers and sisters?
When adult teal fly, they turn in perfect unison and
flash a bright blue patch on their wing.

Pronghorn Antelope Kid

Pronghorn antelope are the fastest mammal in North America. When only four days old, a pronghorn kid can outrun a human! But brand-new babies like this one in southeastern Oregon hide out until they get their running legs.

Red Fox Kits

Fox kits cuddle together to stay warm.
Those large ears you see turn to catch the slightest sounds.
When they're about six weeks old, kits venture out of the den to
play while mom and dad hunt rabbits, birds, or even insects.

Sandpiper Chick

Sandpipers nest on the ground in shallow depressions lined with moss or grass. Both parents sit on the eggs and help raise the young. A chick's bill is at least as long as its head!

Sea Otter Pup

Sea otter babies can float as soon as they are born. Their thick, furry coats act like a sort of life jacket. But the coat doesn't float or keep the pup warm if it's dirty, so mom makes sure her offspring is always well-groomed and fluffy.

Cougar Cub

A cougar cub trains as a predator—stalking, attacking,
and wrestling with its siblings or even with mom. When it grows,
it will leave to hunt on its own. Until then, mom is never far away.

Canada Geese Goslings

KA-RONK! Canada geese are excellent parents, making sure their brood is always very close. Goslings sometimes play at nest building. Tossing dry grass over their shoulders, they tuck pieces around their downy soft bodies creating "make-believe" nests.

I wish to thank Gary Stolz, Chief Naturalist, U.S. Fish and Wildlife Service,
for his invaluable assistance in reviewing yet another manuscript for accuracy. I also wish to thank Mel Calvan,
Chris Eckhoff, Gavriel Jecan, Lisa Pestke, Ray Pfortner, Craig Scheak, and Deirdre Skillman
of my office, for helping to bring this book into the world.
—A. W.

Thanks to my pals, the Burien Library research gals.
For my furry friends: courageous Casey Ben and bright, beautiful Buddy Greenberg. Also for Connie, who
taught me to regard all creatures great and small, and for mom and dad for their enduring love and support.
—A. H.

Published by Sasquatch Books.
Distributed in Canada by Raincoast Books Ltd.
Printed in Hong Kong.
02 01 00 99 98   5 4 3 2 1
Designed by Karen Schober.

Library of Congress Cataloging in Publication Data
Wolfe, Art.
Northwest animal babies/photographs by Art Wolfe; written by Andrea Helman.
p.   cm.
Summary: Introduces some of the baby animals found in the Pacific Northwest, including raccoon kits, a bison calf,
grey wolf pups, Coho salmon fry, Western Sandpiper chicks, and a cougar kitten.
ISBN 1-57061-144-0 (alk. paper)
[1. Animals—Infancy 2. Zoology—Northwest, Pacific.] I. Helman, Andrea, ill. II.Title.
QL 151.W68 1988
591.3'9'09795—dc21   98-5159

Sasquatch Books
615 Second Avenue
Seattle, Washington 98104
(206) 467-4300
books@sasquatchbooks.com
http://www.sasquatchbooks.com

Sasquatch Books publishes high-quality adult nonfiction and children's books related to the Northwest (Alaska to San Francisco).
For more information about our titles, contact us at the address above, or view our site on the World Wide Web.